On a White Pebble Hill

Chyng Feng Sun   Illustrated by Chihsien Chen

Houghton Mifflin Company
Boston 1994

Library of Congress Cataloging-in-Publication Data

Sun, Chyng-Feng.
 On a white pebble hill / by Chyng Feng Sun : illustrated by Chihsien
Chen.
  p.   cm.
 Summary: A young girl takes an imaginary journey through the
various foods on her family's dinner table, where noodle soup
becomes a warm lake with snakes and a roast chicken becomes a golden
mountain.
 ISBN 0-395-68395-5
 [1. Dinners and dining—Fiction. 2. Imagination—Fiction.]
I. Chen, Chihsien, ill.   II. Title.
PZ7.S9565On   1994   93-14495
[E]—dc20   CIP
                       AC

Printed in the United States of America

BP   10   9   8   7   6   5   4   3   2   1

To Mi Miguel
—C.F.S.

For Vivianne with love
—C.C.

Mimi is playing on a hill full of white pebbles.
They're sticky and great for making castles.

She sees a strange lake far away.
"I wish I could go there," she thinks.

She uses the pebbles to make a ball, but when she kicks it . . .

The bird carries her to the lake and drops her in.

Mimi swims happily in the warm water until
she sees the water snakes.

Climbing out of the water, Mimi decides to go exploring.

"Here I go!"

"Why are the flowers so flat?" Mimi wonders.

A huge rock falls from the sky and hits her car.

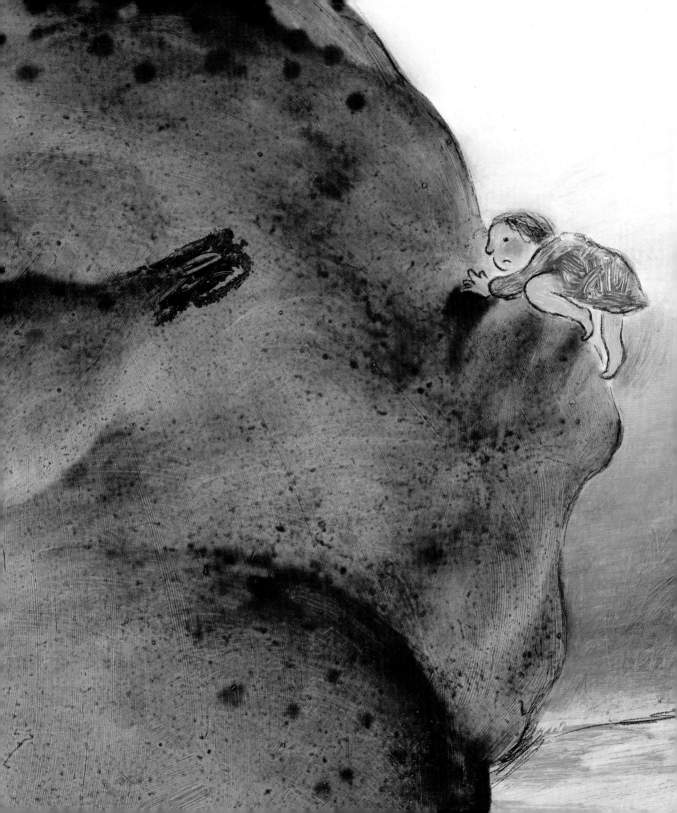

Undiscouraged, Mimi keeps on walking
until a mountain blocks her way.
She climbs up its slippery side.

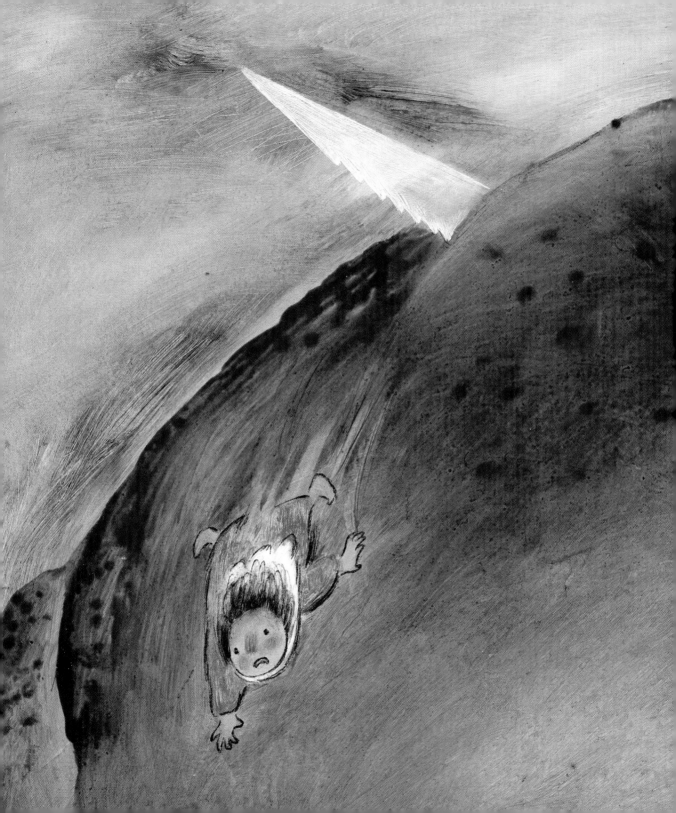

Suddenly the mountain rocks violently.

"Wait! . . . it's really a big chicken!"

"Am I on a giant's dinner table?"

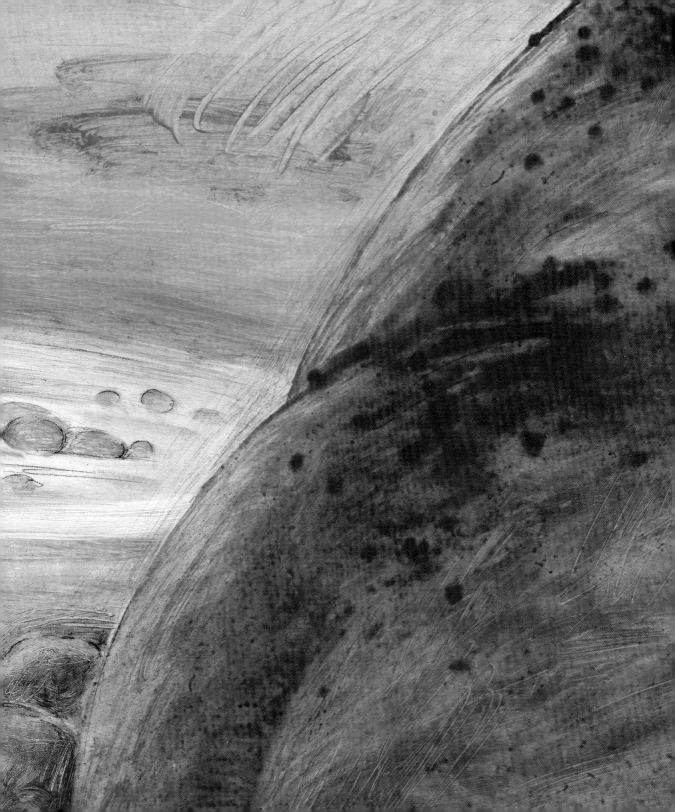

A voice like thunder is coming from the sky.
"Is a giant coming to get me?" Mimi runs to hide.